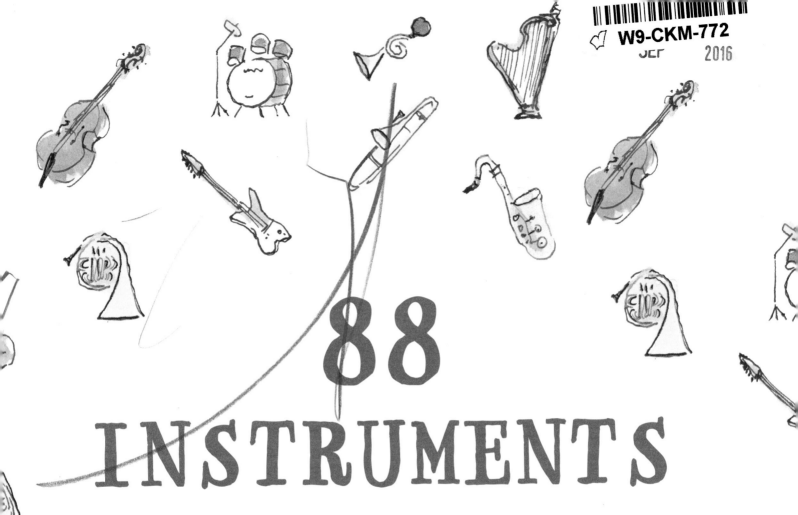

88 INSTRUMENTS

Chris Barton

Illustrations by Louis Thomas

Alfred A. Knopf

New York

For Renée —C.B.
For Anne & Alain —L.T.

THIS IS A BORZOI BOOK PUBLISHED BY ALFRED A. KNOPF

Text copyright © 2016 by Chris Barton
Jacket art and interior illustrations copyright © 2016 by Louis Thomas

All rights reserved. Published in the United States by Alfred A. Knopf, an imprint of
Random House Children's Books, a division of Penguin Random House LLC, New York.

Knopf, Borzoi Books, and the colophon are registered trademarks of Penguin Random House LLC.

Visit us on the Web! randomhousekids.com

Educators and librarians, for a variety of teaching tools, visit us at RHTeachersLibrarians.com

Library of Congress Cataloging-in-Publication Data
Barton, Chris.
88 instruments / Chris Barton; illustrated by Louis Thomas. – First edition.
    pages cm.
Summary: "A little boy can't choose which instrument to play, so he decides to try them all."
—Provided by publisher
ISBN 978-0-553-53814-4 (trade) – ISBN 978-0-553-53815-1 (lib. bdg.) –
ISBN 978-0-553-53823-6 (ebook)
[1. Musical instruments–Fiction. 2. Choice–Fiction.] I. Title. II. Title: Eighty-eight instruments.
PZ7.B2849Aai 2016
[E]—dc23
2015003014

The text of this book is set in 17-point Bodoni Six.

MANUFACTURED IN CHINA
August 2016
10 9 8 7 6 5 4 3 2 1

First Edition

88!

That's how many pounding, surrounding, astounding-mound-of-sounding instruments are in this shop.

But . . . I can take lessons on only one.
Not **75**, or **64**, or **33**, or **12**.
"One," says Dad.
"For now," says Mom.

"Your pick!" says Dad.
"Within reason," says Mom.

How am I supposed to pick just one?

Do I pick the

squeeziest?

The wheeziest?

The easiest and breeziest?

But how about the slideyest . . .

the squonkiest . . .

the blowiest . . .

the
honkiest . . .

the tootiest or grooviest or shiniest?
Or maybe just the tiniest?
There's also the strummiest!
And the thrummiest!

The smashiest! The crashiest!
The drummiest and bashiest!

The twangiest, the rowdiest, the loudiest, the crowdiest, the-

It's so clear.

PLUNK.

So right.

So right *for me*!

I'm going to learn the plinkiest . . .
the plunkiest . . .
and, here to there,
the spunkiest—

the
PIANO!

But wait.

There are *so many* keys to keep straight, so many to master. How many are there?

There's **1**

33

12

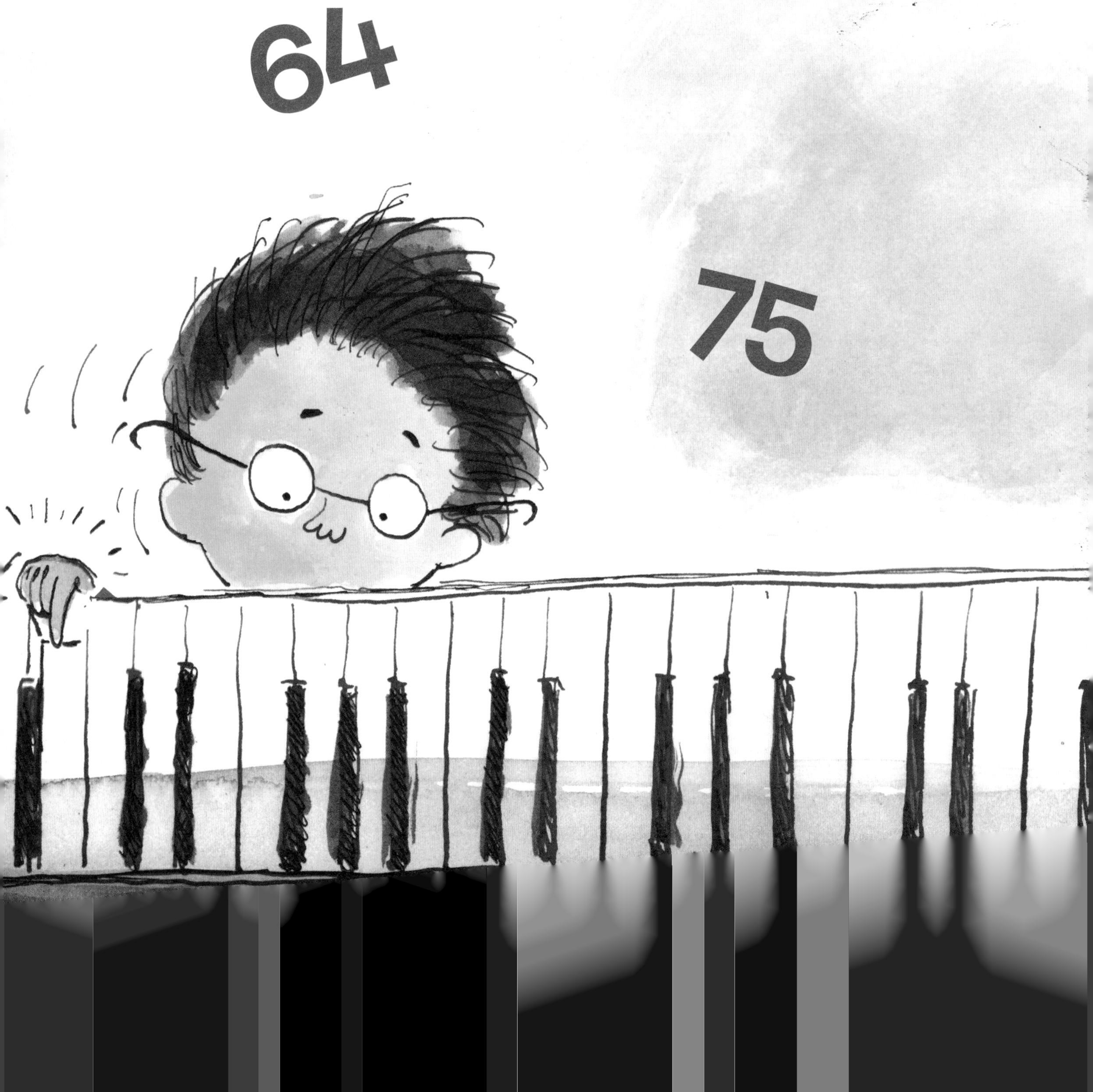
64
75

88 keys, and **88** sounds—
and **88** sounds like a *lot*.

But you know what?

And soon I'll be ready for all **88.**